SCAREDY CATS

For Briony and Mike
who are mad about cats!

**Find out more about the Scaredy Cats
at Shoo's fabulous website:
www.shoo-rayner.co.uk**

ORCHARD BOOKS
338 Euston Road,
London NW1 3BH
Orchard Books Australia
Hachette Children's Books
Level 17/207 Kent Street, Sydney, NSW 2000
First published in Great Britain in 2004
First paperback edition 2005
Copyright © Shoo Rayner 2004
The right of Shoo Rayner to be identified as the author
and illustrator of this work has been asserted by him in
accordance with the Copyright, Designs, and Patents Act, 1988.
A CIP catalogue record for this book is available
from the British Library.
ISBN 978 1 84362 731 9
1 3 5 7 9 10 8 6 4 2 (hardback)
3 5 7 9 10 8 6 4 (paperback)
Printed in Great Britain

Catula

ORCHARD BOOKS

Daisy the dentist's cat sneaked out through the back door. She had heard the noise and couldn't get away fast enough.

Daisy's heart thumped as she fled
down the main street, darting between
the shadows.

Eight cats were waiting for her at the secret circle. They were the other members of the secret society of Scaredy Cats.

"I heard *the* noise!" Daisy's voice squeaked with nerves. "They've been up in the attic and brought down THE BASKET!"

The whole group gasped, "It's the vet for you tomorrow, then!"

Daisy trembled with fear.

Kipling's eyes narrowed into slits.
Silence fell upon the secret circle.
Kipling was ready to tell a story. The
story they had all come to hear.

"You'd better pray that your vet isn't like the terrible Dr Catula," growled Kipling, their leader.

"We've all been to the vet and know what it's like," Kipling began. "All that prodding and poking and the horrible smell of medicines."

"When the vet reaches into your basket and pulls you out, what's the one thing you want to do?"

"Bite him! Scratch him!" the Scaredy Cats howled their reply.

Kipling purred and licked his lips —
"Well, once there was a vet whose
name struck terror in the hearts of
cats throughout the land. His name
was Dr Catula."

Given the chance, even the weakest cat would sink their teeth into his flesh. But Dr Catula's grip never weakened. He just smiled at their owners and said that it didn't hurt.

And it didn't hurt! Dr Catula didn't
feel the pain anymore. So many teeth
and claws had mixed with his blood
that strange things had happened to
his body.

At dusk, under the evening stars, he'd change. His nails turned into claws, and his eyes flashed green as emeralds.

With pointy ears and a long,
swishing tail, he sloped across rooftops
and shimmied down drainpipes.

Skulking in dark, damp cellars, he hunted rats and mice, which he saved in his pockets for later.

Only when he was back in the
safety of his surgery would he crunch
their furry little bodies. Then he'd
snuggle down to sleep in front of the
radiator, purring his strange, husky,
human purr.

But small, furry animals were not
enough for Dr Catula. To stay alive,
he had to drink the blood of cats!
One day, my Aunt Bella, a beautiful
Persian cat, was brought to Dr Catula.

Bella's owners were worried about her. She had a cough that sounded like a dog's bark!

"I'll need a blood sample," said Dr Catula, as he dragged Bella from her basket. "I'll do a test to make sure that Bella hasn't got cat flu."

Behind a screen, Dr Catula tested
Bella's blood in his own special way.

"Mmmmm! Delicious!" he muttered
as he smacked his lips. His eyes
glittered excitedly as he spoke to Bella's
owners. "Bella could be very ill. I'd like
to keep her over night so I can do
more tests."

In the hot, stuffy ward, the other animals told Bella the whole truth about Dr Catula.

"He'll keep you here until he's had every last drop of your cat blood!" a dog with a broken leg told her.

"It's true!" said a featherless parrot. "I've seen him doing it at night."

"You must try to escape," implored a rabbit with bent ears. "Quickly… before he comes back for you. Then it will be too late."

Bella clawed helplessly at the stout
lock on her cage. Panic made her
cough worse and soon she was
fighting for every breath.

She was exhausted by the time
Dr Catula came looking for his supper.
His hands trembled with excitement
as he lifted Bella out of the cage.

Dr Catula held her tight with one hand as he prepared the instruments with his other.

Bella felt a cool breeze from a half-open window. The cold night air made her throat tickle. When Bella coughed, she sounded like a guard dog about to attack!

R-r-ruff!

Dr Catula was so surprised, he
loosened his grip for a split second. It
was enough. Bella bounded through
the window in a flash.

But Dr Catula was right behind her.
He crashed through the window and
chased after her as she ran for her life.

Fighting for every breath, Bella ran
for the safety of the nearest tree and
scrambled to the very top branch.

But Dr Catula was half-man,
half-cat. Slowly, carefully, he climbed
up after her, smiling wickedly. The
moonlight glistened on his fangs
— Bella was trapped.

Panting — clinging to the end of the
furthest branch — Bella's body was
shaken with an uncontrollable fit of
coughing.

She lost her balance and fell. Bella twisted and turned, grabbing and clawing at thin air. A leafy branch slapped her in the face. She clung to it desperately.

As she hung in the air, gasping for breath, something crashed through the branches above her.

Trying to grab Bella as she fell,
Dr Catula had lost his balance too.
Bella never forgot the look of terror
in his glittering, cat-like eyes as he
fell past her.

It was the human body of Dr
Catula that was found under the tree.
People assumed he'd been trying to
save the pretty Persian cat that was
stuck in the branches above him.

On Dr Catula's gravestone they carved some very special words.

Dr Catula.

He died as he lived, trying to save the lives of animals.

The shocked silence of the Scaredy Cat's circle was broken by a voice. "Daisy! Daisy!"

Daisy looked at her friends. "They're calling me. I'd better go."

As they watched Daisy creep back home, Freddy called after her, "Give the vet a really good bite from me tomorrow!"

Freddy turned to Kipling, "That couldn't happen in real life, could it?" he asked.

Kipling raised an eyebrow and smiled. "Couldn't it? You'll have to ask my Aunt Bella."

SCAREDY CATS

Shoo Rayner

❏ Frankatstein	1 84362 729 9	£3.99
❏ Foggy Moggy Inn	1 84362 730 2	£3.99
❏ Catula	1 84362 731 0	£3.99
❏ Catkin Farm	1 84362 732 9	£3.99
❏ Bluebeard's Cat	1 84362 733 7	£3.99
❏ The Killer Catflap	1 84362 744 2	£3.99
❏ Dr Catkyll and Mr Hyde	1 84362 745 0	£3.99
❏ Catnapped	1 84362 746 9	£3.99

Little HORRORS

❏ The Swamp Man	1 84121 646 1	£3.99
❏ The Pumpkin Man	1 84121 644 5	£3.99
❏ The Spider Man	1 84121 648 8	£3.99
❏ The Sand Man	1 84121 650 X	£3.99
❏ The Shadow Man	1 84362 021 X	£3.99
❏ The Bone Man	1 84362 010 3	£3.99
❏ The Snow Man	1 84362 009 X	£3.99
❏ The Bogey Man	1 84362 011 1	£3.99